MW01107639

Tales of American Folklore

Perfection Learning®

Retold by Peg Hall

Editor: Paula J. Reece
Illustrator: Michael A. Aspengren

For information, contact
Perfection Learning® Corporation
1000 North Second Avenue, P.O. Box 500
Logan, Iowa 51546-0500.
Phone: 1-800-831-4190 • Fax: 1-712-644-2392

PB ISBN-10: 0-7891-5218-5 ISBN-13: 978-0-7891-5218-3
RLB ISBN-10: 0-7807-9673-x ISBN-13: 978-0-7807-9673-7
Printed in the U.S.A.

6 7 8 9 10 11 PP 13 12 11 10 09 08

Table of Contents

Johnny Appleseed

There were two things young John Chapman loved. One was animals. And the other was apple trees.

John was born in Boston on a wild and rainy spring day. Some tell a story about his birth. They say that as soon as Johnny took his first breath, the storm stopped. The sun came out and splashed a rainbow across the sky. And that rainbow ended right at the door of the Chapman house.

No one knows whether or not *that* story's true. But right from the start, it was clear that the boy was special. He had some kind of magic to him. Wild animals would come right out of the forest to visit him. Sick and hurt creatures would heal at Johnny's touch.

But it wasn't just the animals that felt Johnny's magic. Plants did too. In fact, anything that Johnny stuck in the dirt soon grew tall and strong.

Maybe that gift is what got Johnny started planting apple seeds. Or maybe it was the notion that there wasn't anything better than apple trees. And that there shouldn't be any place where they didn't grow.

Whatever the reason, it's a good thing Johnny did what he did. Without him, there might not be any apples west of the great Mississippi River.

You see, Johnny lived during an itchy time. People were on the move from east to west. It seemed like every day another family packed up and headed off. They went to find new land and new dreams. They went to seek adventure and riches. They went just to see what was out there.

And sometimes one or two would come back. They'd tell tales of all the things they had seen.

One day when Johnny was just about grown, he met a man who changed his life. Johnny was hard at work in the family orchard. He was happily picking apples when the man came by.

"I'd give a lot for one of them apples, boy," the man called.

Johnny laughed and tossed an apple to the man. "You can have it for nothing," he said.

The man stopped to eat the apple. In between bites, he told his story. He had been out to the West. Now he was back to get his family. They were going to settle out there.

"It's a great place, son," said the man. "Though I sure do miss apples. You don't see any apple trees out there."

"Well, then," said Johnny. "Take some seeds with you. Plant them and you'll soon have your own apples."

"That's a fine thought," said the man. "I'll do it."

That gave Johnny an idea. He could give apple seeds to people who were headed to the West. If they each planted a few seeds, soon orchards would bloom there. There would be apples for everyone.

So that's what Johnny started doing. He collected seeds from apples that fell on the ground. He went through the mash left after making cider and picked out the seeds. Before long he had a leather bag filled with seeds.

Of course, people thought he was a bit crazy. The boy talked to animals, after all. And he picked up seeds everywhere he went. What else could people think?

None of that bothered Johnny. He didn't care what other people thought. He only cared about two things. One was animals. The other was apple trees.

But after a while Johnny began to think he wasn't doing enough. He didn't know if anyone actually planted the seeds he sent west with them. The only way he could be sure was to plant them himself.

So Johnny outfitted himself for the West. He was a simple man, so he didn't need much. He put a beat-up, old pot on his head to keep off the hot sun. He made a traveling suit by cutting holes in an old feed sack. Then he put his bag of seeds over one shoulder and set out.

Johnny walked the whole way. (Except when he had to cross the Ohio River.) He walked for hundreds and hundreds of miles. Most of the time, he was barefoot. It didn't matter if it rained or snowed. Johnny didn't mind.

As he traveled, Johnny handed out apple seeds. He told people to plant them.

Every so often, Johnny would settle somewhere for a spell. That was whenever someone gave him a piece of land to use. Then Johnny would plant seeds himself. He'd start a new orchard and gather a new supply of seeds. Soon there were apple trees all over Ohio and Indiana.

It was hard work, but Johnny was happy. He became known far and wide as "Johnny Appleseed." Stories about him were heard everywhere.

One of those stories was about Johnny and some bugs. It seems that one night Johnny made a fire. But before long he noticed little sparks blazing up and falling into the flames. He saw that the sparks were bugs. The creatures were drawn to the flames. But when they got close, the heat set their wings on fire.

Well, Johnny wasn't about to let that happen. Even to a bug. So right away he put that fire out. He slept in the cold that night and every night afterward.

Another time Johnny crawled into a big hollow log to sleep. As he went in, he heard a snort and a grumble. There was a big brown bear in the log!

That didn't bother Johnny, of course. He just said, "Excuse me, Brother Bear." The surprise is that it didn't seem to bother the bear either. The two of them just cuddled up for the night inside that log.

But best of all is the story about Johnny and the wolf. It seems that one day Johnny was picking herbs. He heard a low howl just ahead.

It was a sad howl, the howl of an animal in trouble. So Johnny had to go look. He found a great black wolf with its paw stuck in a steel trap.

Another man might have shot that wolf. Another man might just have left quietly the way he came. But not Johnny. He walked right up to the wolf. Without a care for himself, he reached down and pulled off the trap. Then he wrapped a cloth around the hurt paw.

From then on, Johnny and the wolf were always together. When Johnny set out to walk, the wolf followed. When Johnny lay down to sleep, the wolf curled up next to him. Some even say the wolf would use its paws to dig holes for Johnny's seeds.

The two of them traveled all over this great country. They traveled all the way to the Rocky Mountains. And in each place they stopped, an apple orchard would later spring up.

Johnny and the wolf went on this way for years. After a while Johnny's hair turned gray, and his step slowed a bit. The wolf's fur grew gray, and its eyes dimmed. Still they walked on.

Until one day a farmer saw the wolf. The

man hadn't heard about Johnny and his wolf. Quick as a flash, he raised his rifle. Quick as a flash, he shot that wolf.

Johnny was heartbroken. He sat for a long time beside his dead friend. At last he buried the wolf by the side of a stream. He planted his best apple seeds at the edges of the grave. No one is sure where the spot is now. But some say the apple trees grow thicker there than anywhere else.

After that Johnny went on alone. He missed the wolf, but he was happy in his work. Everywhere he went, orchards sprang up.

"That Johnny Appleseed," people would say. "He's crazy!"

Johnny didn't care. He just walked on. Until finally the day came when he was too tired to walk anymore.

Johnny lay down in a small orchard. He looked up at the branches overhead. Then he closed his eyes. His work was done.

The next day a traveler found Johnny's body. Around him was a quiet circle of animals.

Johnny was buried in that orchard. But his work lives on in every apple seed that gets planted. In every apple tree that blossoms and bears fruit. And in every crisp apple that gets eaten.

Stormalong

No one's too sure where Stormalong was born. People think it was somewhere down East like Nantucket or Kennebunk or Kittery. Some place where the winters were long and the summers were short. A place where the soil grew rocks instead of wheat. A place so full of hardship that lots of young men took to the sea. Just like Stormalong did.

It all started when a ship called the *Sea Maid* came to port. She was going to take lumber, furs, and cotton cloth to China. Her captain was looking for a good crew. Still, he was a bit surprised when Stormalong showed up.

"I think I want to be a cabin boy," Stormalong said.

"You?" said the captain. He looked at Stormy, who was about two fathoms high at the time. And since a fathom is about six feet, that's big for a cabin boy.

So the captain said, "You're kind of big for a cabin boy. Just how old are you?"

"Twelve-going-on-thirteen," said Stormy. "At least, that's what they tell me."

"Well, that's the right age for a cabin boy," said the captain. "Are you strong and healthy?"

"I'm strong enough, I guess," answered Stormy. "I can throw a codfish farther than anyone else. At least, that's what they tell me. And I'm never sick."

"Well, then, you just might do," said the captain.

So Stormalong signed up to be a cabin boy. He wrote his name like this: *Stormalong, A.B.* That's because his full name was Albert Bulltop Stormalong.

The captain looked at the book and thought, *A.B.*? Well that makes sense. He's big. And he's sure able-bodied.

Ever since, sailors have written the letters *A.B.* after their names.

So the *Sea Maid* took to the sea with

Stormalong on board. The rest of the crew liked the new cabin boy. But his size was a problem. Stormy was still a growing boy. He ate more than any six sailors. Before long he was four fathoms tall. He was so big that he made the ship tip to one side when he walked across the deck.

Stormalong quickly learned all he needed to know about being a sailor. He got to like eating salt pork and beef jerky. He could look at a ship far away and know just what kind it was. He could climb up the mast to the crow's nest in a matter of seconds. And he could tie every sailor's knot that had ever been tied.

It was his knot tying that first made Stormalong famous.

One sky blue day the *Sea Maid* was sailing at full speed. All of a sudden the ship stopped dead in the water. It stopped so fast that the cook's pots all clattered to the floor. Sailors on the deck went sliding along until they could grab something. And men who were sleeping in their bunks got tossed out.

Wind filled the *Sea Maid*'s sails. The ship creaked and groaned. But it didn't move.

"What's the trouble?" asked Stormalong.

"Has to be a kraken," said one of the oldest sailors. He had been a seaman his whole life. He knew all there was to know.

"A kraken?" said Stormalong. "What's a kraken?"

"Well," said the seaman. "I almost hate to tell you, sonny. That's how fearful the beast is. You see, it's like an octopus. But it has more arms. It's the biggest, meanest, most powerful monster ever to live in the deep blue sea. And now it's got the *Sea Maid* in its clutches."

"What are we going to do?" asked the captain.

Nobody said anything. Nobody did anything. So Stormalong kicked off his shoes and dived overboard.

Stormy swam down, down, down into the black water. Before long he could see the keel of the ship. A long arm was wrapped around it. The arm was covered with great suckers. Each sucker was stuck to the ship like glue.

Stormy's eyes followed that arm all the way to the other end of the beast. The kraken had a big, lumpy head. It had two mean-looking eyes. And it had at least 12 other arms, all waving wildly.

Well, it's a kraken for sure, thought Stormalong. Unless it's something worse.

But he didn't spend a lot of time thinking. He grabbed hold of the kraken's arm and started pulling. He pulled, and he pulled. The suckers on the arm came loose. *POP! POP! POP!* A rush of bubbles rose through the water.

Stormy got the kraken's arm off the ship. But it just wrapped another arm around the keel.

Then Stormy got an idea. He grabbed one of the beast's loose arms. Quick as a wink, he tied it up in a bowline knot. Then he tied another in a half hitch. He kept on going, tying every knot he'd ever learned. And even some he hadn't.

The kraken rolled and wrestled. But it was no match for Stormalong. Soon it only had one arm free—the one holding the ship. With a great heave, the kraken lifted that arm toward Stormalong. But before it could get him, Stormy tied the arm in a reef knot.

Finally the tangled-up kraken had had enough. It gave Stormy one last hateful look. Then it slid off, even deeper into the sea.

Stormalong swam to the surface. There he found that the ship was heaving and dipping. His fight with the kraken had set the sea churning in great waves.

Still, everyone cheered when Stormy climbed aboard. And before long the *Sea Maid* was once again on its way to China.

When the trip was over, the captain offered Stormy a job. "You can sign on as a sailor," he said. "Even if you're not really old enough."

"Thanks," said Stormy. "But I think I need to find a bigger ship, captain. I'm kind of outgrowing this one."

Now while the *Sea Maid* had been gone, a war had broken out. The Revolutionary War, to be exact. And America had put together a navy to fight against the English. John Paul Jones was in charge of all the ships.

So Stormalong joined the navy. It's a good thing too. Without him, America might not have won the war.

In one battle, things didn't go well for John Paul Jones. An English ship shot a big hole in the side of his ship.

"We've got trouble!" John Paul Jones shouted.

Stormalong looked things over. "We could be sinking," he said. "Let's get closer to the English ship."

John Paul Jones was no fool. He just turned his ship over to Stormalong. Stormy steered the American ship right into the English ship. The whole American crew jumped aboard. They took the ship away from the Englishmen. Then they went on to capture *another* English ship.

By the time the war ended, Stormalong had reached his full growth. Now even a warship really wasn't a comfortable fit. But Stormalong had an idea. "I'll build me a clipper ship," he said. "A ship just the right size for someone like me."

So Stormalong set to work. He worked with a couple hundred other men. They spent the next three years in the shipyard.

Along the way, they used up most of the lumber in the country. In fact, for a while no one could find enough wood to build a house.

The sails were so big that there was nowhere to spread them out for stitching. They had to be taken all the way to the Sahara Desert.

The ship's masts were so tall that they scraped against the clouds. Stormalong solved that problem by making them so they could fold down.

At last the ship was done. Stormalong called her the *Courser*.

All clipper ships are fast. Speed is what they're known for. But the *Courser* was the fastest of all. It could sail from one end of the ocean to another in a matter of days. It went all over—to China, India, and Europe.

However, the *Courser*'s size was sometimes a problem. It was too big to anchor close to the shore. Cargo had to be loaded into smaller boats and brought in that way.

The wheel of the boat was huge. Stormy

could handle it. But when he wasn't on duty, it took 32 men to turn the thing!

And then there was the time Stormalong decided to sail through the English Channel. The channel is only about 20 miles wide. So was the *Courser*.

That didn't stop Stormalong. He just called to his men, "Grab bars of soap, boys. Rub them all along the sides of the ship. Make it good and thick!"

The crew set to work. In no time at all, the sides of the ship were white with soap.

As Stormalong steered into the channel, the black cliffs rose on both sides. The men held their breaths. One side of the *Courser* scraped against the cliff. Then the other. But Stormalong kept going.

His plan worked! The soap let the *Courser* slip through the narrow channel. Of course, some soap scraped off onto the cliffs. That's why they're white now. If you don't believe it, go and see for yourself.

Stormalong's troubles on this journey weren't over yet. After going through the channel, the *Courser* got into shallow water. The bottom of the ship was scraping along the ocean floor.

"We have to throw the cargo overboard, captain!" shouted one sailor.

"Save the cargo!" shouted Stormalong. "Throw the ballast into the water!"

So the men went down into the bottom of the ship. They started carrying out all the rocks and stones that weighed the ship down.

Because the *Courser* was so big, it had a lot of ballast. So much was thrown overboard that it made islands in the sea. They're still there to this day.

A short time later Stormalong got bored with carrying cargo. So he went into whaling. These were the great days of whaling. People all over the world used whale oil and whale bone for all kinds of things.

Stormy liked the idea that whales were so big. Big enough to put up a bit of a fight—even against someone his size. So he took the *Courser* out after every kind of whale anybody had ever heard of. He went after white whales and gray whales. He went after finbacks and humpbacks. He even went after the blue whale—the biggest creature of all.

Stormalong loved whaling. He loved chasing whales. He loved catching them. But most of all, he loved eating whale steaks. So he was happy with his new life.

Until something came along that worried him.

Steamships!

Every year there were more and more of them. Every year they got bigger and faster. Then one day the impossible happened. A steamship called the *Liverpool Packet* went racing past the *Courser!*

Stormalong was beside himself! He stormed about on the deck. He stamped his feet so hard that he almost sank his own ship!

Stormalong decided to have a race. It would be between the *Courser* and the *Liverpool Packet.* And the *Courser* would win!

First Stormalong had to find the *Liverpool Packet.* He hung around in open water, waiting. And waiting.

At last the steamship came into sight. It was headed for Boston.

"I'll beat you to Boston!" shouted Stormalong to the captain of the *Liverpool Packet.* "Or I'll die trying!"

"You don't have a chance!" the captain shouted back. "There's no wind! And you don't have steam!" Then the *Liverpool Packet* raced past.

Two days later Stormalong and his boat were still sitting on the water. There was no wind. The boat wasn't going anywhere.

At last a puff of wind came up. Then a real

blow started up. The sails began to shake. They filled with wind.

The *Courser* shot across the water. Before long it had caught up with the *Liverpool Packet*. It sailed on by in a spray of foam.

No one knows exactly what happened next. Some say Stormy just kept going north. Some say they saw the *Courser* the next day, its sails tattered and torn. Some say Stormy went on to sail a great ship in the sky.

"Sailors come, and sailors go," said one old sea salt. "But Stormy was the best. Aye, we'll never forget him."

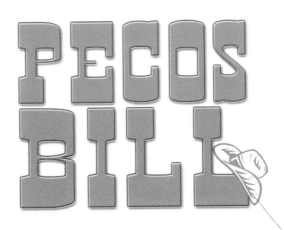

PECOS BILL

The deeds of Pecos Bill have been sung about for years. Never was there a cowboy like Bill—before or since.

Bill was born in Texas, in the Pecos River valley. This was back when hardly anyone lived there.

Bill's folks were tough, as settlers had to be. His mother once chased off 45 Indians. She was only armed with a broom handle, which tells you a lot about her.

Bill's father didn't think much of people. When Bill was one year old, someone moved in just 50 miles to the east. "It's too crowded for me here," said Bill's father. "Time for us to move on."

So Bill's folks loaded up a big wagon and set off to the West. It was a noisy trip because there were more than a dozen children in the family. It was so noisy that no one noticed when young Bill fell out of the wagon. In fact, he wasn't missed for weeks. And by then, it was too late.

So there was Bill, sitting in the dirt. He sat for a long time, just looking around. Then a whole pack of coyotes came by.

Well, the coyotes had never seen a human before. So they thought maybe Bill was a strange coyote with no fur. One coyote brought the boy a hunk of meat. From then on, Bill was a member of the pack.

Bill learned to talk like a coyote. He learned to hunt and run on all fours and howl at the moon.

Bill was about ten years old before he saw another human. A cowboy came along just as Bill picked a fight with a bear. The cowboy watched while Bill squeezed the bear to death.

Then the cowboy looked Bill over from head to toe. "Why aren't you wearing clothes, boy?" he asked.

Of course, Bill didn't understand a word the cowboy said. He only knew how to talk like a coyote. So he growled a bit and scratched behind one ear with his leg.

Then the cowboy threw Bill something to eat. That pleased Bill, so he decided not to bite the man.

The cowboy spent three days with Bill. He taught him how to talk like a human being. And he tried to make Bill see that he was a human himself.

"No, I'm not," said Bill. "I'm a coyote. I can run and hunt and howl. I'm no human."

"Then why don't you have a tail?" asked the cowboy. "All your coyote friends have tails."

Bill turned around and stared at his rear end. Sure enough, there was no tail to be seen. "I've never noticed that before," said Bill. "But you're right. I must be a human after all."

Bill wasn't too sure he liked the idea of being human. But it was plain to see that he was. So he went with the cowboy to the next town.

After a while Bill got to liking the idea of being human. But he started running around with a bad crowd. Before long Bill was pretty wild.

For a time Bill worked as an outlaw. He invented the six-shooter. He came up with the idea of robbing trains and banks. Soon Bill was famous all through the West.

But then Bill decided to move on. He saddled up his horse and headed even farther west. He was looking for a hard-riding, hard-talking bunch of cowboys.

After about 100 miles, Bill's horse broke its leg. Bill had to go on foot, carrying his saddle in one hand.

All at once Bill came across a huge rattlesnake. The snake lifted its head. It hissed and shook its rattles.

Bill wanted to be fair, so he let the snake have three bites. Then he picked the thing up by the tail. He started spinning it in loops over his head. He set off again. His saddle was in one hand. The spinning snake was in the other. Before long Bill was roping Gila monsters.

About 50 miles farther along, Bill met a big mountain lion. This wasn't your usual lion. It was as big as three steers. It was meaner than a cross-eyed bear. And it smelled worse than a whole passel of skunks.

But Bill just laughed at the mountain lion. He dropped his saddle and the snake. Then he let the lion have it. Fur flew through the air. So much fur that daylight wasn't seen in those parts for a full week.

After about three minutes, the lion gave up. Then Bill put the saddle on the lion's back. He hopped on and went down the canyon, riding that lion. He used the rattlesnake as a whip. The mountain lion jumped about a hundred feet at a time, but it couldn't throw Bill.

Before long Bill met up with a bunch of cowboys. They were sitting around a campfire by their wagon. They were a bit surprised to see Bill ride up on the lion. They were even more surprised to see the rattlesnake in his hand.

Bill pulled on the lion's ear to get it to stop. Then

he stepped off and hung the snake around his neck.

Bill looked those cowboys over. No one said anything.

Bill grabbed a pan of beans off the campfire. He swallowed the beans and washed them down with a gallon of coffee.

When he was done, Bill wiped his mouth. He asked, "Who's the boss here?"

The biggest cowboy got to his feet. He took off his hat and said, "I was, mister. But I guess you are now."

Bill liked the sound of that, so he decided to stay. He had lots of adventures with this group. In fact, it was while he was with them that he found his horse. *Widow-maker* was the horse's name. Bill was the only man who could ride him.

In fact, there wasn't a horse Bill couldn't ride. He was thrown once. But that wasn't by a horse. It was by a tornado.

You see, Bill made a bet that he could ride a tornado—without a saddle. Then he went off to Kansas to find one. Not just any tornado, mind you. This was the worst windstorm ever seen.

Bill hopped up on that tornado's back. Then the thing started bucking and pitching and trying to throw Bill off. It roared up mountains and down valleys. It tied rivers into knots and dug huge holes in the ground. It knocked down so many trees that there was nothing left of Kansas except bare prairie.

But it couldn't throw Bill off. He just sat there, hitting the tornado in the side with his hat. Whooping and hollering and having himself a grand old time.

The tornado roared through three states, but Bill stayed on its back. In Arizona, the tornado decided to rain itself out from under him. So much water gushed out that the Grand Canyon was formed. And when Bill finally fell to the ground, he made a hole a hundred feet deep. Today we call that *Death Valley*. You can still see the print of his jeans in the rocky floor of the valley.

Bill was also known as a great roper. He actually invented the art of cattle roping. As you know, he started with his rattlesnake. Then he moved on to a rope so long that he could lasso a whole herd of cows with one throw.

This skill came in handy when one of Bill's pals got in trouble. It seems the fellow decided to ride Widow-maker. The horse didn't take to the idea. It threw him all the way up to the top of Pike's Peak. And if Bill hadn't been such a great roper, the man would have stayed up there.

But Bill just made a great lasso out of his rope. Then he tossed it 20,000 feet up and around his pal's neck. One pull and the fellow was back down in the valley below.

Of course, a man like Bill was liked by the ladies. But Bill's heart belonged to Slue-Foot Sue. He fell in love with her the first time he saw her. Sue was riding a catfish down the Rio Grande River. Back then, catfish were bigger than whales. So Bill was mighty impressed.

Bill and Sue got married. But Sue made a bad mistake on their wedding day. She kept at Bill until he let her ride Widow-maker. The horse threw her so high that the moon had to duck.

When Sue came back down to earth, her wide skirts made her bounce. Every time she hit the ground, she bounced back up again. Poor Bill ran along after her, begging her to settle down.

Sue bounced for three days and four nights. But at last she came down to stay. After that Bill and Sue were happy for many years.

There are many stories about how Bill met his end. Some say his drinking did him in. Some say it was his habit of eating barbed wire. It seems the wire rusted in his stomach and killed him.

But some say it was meeting a fellow from Boston that caused Bill's death. The man showed up in a mail-order cowboy suit. He started asking stupid questions about the West. Poor Bill lay himself down and laughed until he died.

Paul Bunyan

Lumberjacks were big, strong men. But Paul Bunyan was the biggest and strongest of all. He was so big that he used a pine tree to comb his beard. He was so strong that he could drive a tree stump into the ground with his fist.

Of course, Paul was a lot smaller when he was a baby in Maine. But he was still bigger than any baby was supposed to be. In fact, some folks say that baby Paul's size got him thrown out of the state. The people were a bit worried. It seems that baby Paul knocked down miles of trees every time he rolled over.

Paul's folks thought they had a way to solve the problem. They made a big cradle out of the trees Paul had knocked down. Then they set it out in the bay.

Everything was all right for a while. Until Paul started to wiggle. The cradle rocked back and forth. Soon great waves were washing up on the shore.

That's when Paul's family was asked to leave. Everyone wanted Paul out of Maine before he did some serious damage.

No one knows exactly where Paul and his family went next. But we do know that Paul showed up years later in Wisconsin. Or it might have been Minnesota. Somewhere with a lot of trees. And he became a lumberjack.

Naturally, Paul was no ordinary lumberjack. There was the time that he dug a river. This happened in Minnesota for sure. Paul was cutting trees there. And he had to get them all the way to New Orleans.

The easiest way to do that would be to float the logs south. But there was no river that went from Minnesota to New Orleans.

So Paul did some thinking. While he thought, he ate a snack. Nothing much. Just 3 hams, 10 loaves of bread, 150 pancakes, and 5 gallons of cider.

But that gave Paul enough strength to dig. He dug the river that very afternoon. All the way from Minnesota to New Orleans. He called it the Mississippi.

Paul's also the one who set up the state of Iowa for farming. You see, the place was covered with trees—everywhere. There was hardly a patch of bare ground to be seen.

Then Paul showed up. He took a couple of

practice swings and cleared half the state. Then he really got to work. By the time he stopped, Iowa was cleared from border to border. But Paul had gotten a bit carried away. There wasn't a tree left in North Dakota or Kansas either.

The farmers thanked Paul. Then they got busy planting corn and wheat.

As you can imagine, Paul's logging camps were big. In fact, the crew had a bunkhouse with a hinged chimney. That's because it was so tall that the moon would scrape against it at night.

The dining hall was so long that you couldn't see from one end to another. And the food? Well, it took a lot of food to feed Paul and his crew.

That's why Paul's blacksmith made a huge iron pot for the new kitchen. It held 1,000 gallons of soup. The thing was so big that the cook had to use a rowboat when he made soup. He'd row out into the middle and dump in potatoes, cabbage, and meat.

But Paul's favorite meal was pancakes. So he wanted a big pancake griddle too. The blacksmith made a griddle so big that it covered ten acres of land.

The griddle was too big for the cook to handle. So he called for some helpers. They each strapped slabs of bacon to their feet. Then they skated out onto the griddle.

As they moved over the hot iron, the bacon

melted. After a while it would get so steamy that they couldn't see. Then the cook knew it was time to make the pancakes.

Of course, the pancakes were bigger than normal too. They were so huge that it took four or five men to eat just one. Except for Paul. He could eat a dozen all by himself.

Paul had himself a special friend too. He found his friend one cold winter. It snowed and snowed and snowed that year. It was so cold that Paul's nose turned blue. It was so cold that the *snow* was blue!

Of course, the cold didn't bother Paul. So he went out for a walk. He hadn't gotten far when he tripped over something in the snow.

Well, Paul wondered what was there. After all, it had to be pretty big to trip *him* up. So he started digging.

Before long he uncovered a tail. He kept on digging. And he found something amazing at the other end. It was an ox—a blue ox!

It was easy to see that the ox was a baby. Still, it was half as big as Paul. So Paul carried the poor thing back to camp to warm it up.

Once they got near the fire, Paul's nose got back to normal. But the ox stayed blue. That didn't bother Paul. He decided to keep the ox. And he named his ox Babe.

Babe kept on growing. Before he stopped, his

horns were 42 ax handles wide. He was so heavy that he left footprints in solid rock. And he ate so much that it took a whole crew of lumberjacks just to haul his food to camp.

But Babe was a big help too. It didn't take Paul and his crew long to chop down all the trees in an area. Then they'd have to move on. But they didn't have to build a new logging camp. Paul would just hitch the buildings to Babe. Then the big blue ox would drag everything along with him.

They cleared a lot of land that way too.

Then there was the time that Paul and his crew were working in Wisconsin. The road between the camp and where they were logging was very twisty. It was so twisty that men going to work met themselves coming back!

Paul didn't like this much. It took the men far too long to get to work on such a twisty road. So he hitched Babe up to one end of the road.

Babe gave a couple of tugs. He huffed and puffed once or twice. Then *PING!* That road snapped like a rubber band. Then it lay down nice and straight like a road should.

No one knows what happened to Paul and Babe. Some say they finished their work. Then they went into the woods to take a nap.

It could be that they're still there.

JOHN HENRY

John Henry was born to be a steel-driving man. Why, when he was little more than a boy, John Henry could swing a hammer. He could swing it higher and faster than a grown man could.

But there wasn't any steel driving for John Henry. Not at first. He spent his days picking cotton on his master's plantation. He spent his nights listening to the *click-clack* of trains carrying Southern soldiers to battle. And he dreamed about driving steel.

John Henry told his mama and papa about his dreams. "I'm not surprised," said his papa. "It's plain to see that you were born to be a steel-driving man."

"There's more," said John Henry. "I dreamed that I'd die with a hammer in my hand."

John Henry's words worried his mama and papa. But they knew their boy was safe with them. And after a while they forgot what he had said.

However, John Henry never forgot his dream of driving steel. Not even when he got to be full-grown. Not even when he fell in love with sweet Polly Ann.

Not even when he made her his bride. And not even when Polly Ann gave him a fine, strapping son.

Then the Civil War ended. The slaves were free. At last men like John Henry could do what they wanted. And John Henry knew what *that* was.

To the west, men were building a great railroad that would cross the country. So John Henry said to his wife, "Polly Ann, we have to go west. For I was born to be a steel-driving man."

John Henry, Polly Ann, and their baby left the very next day. As they walked, John Henry thought, there's a hammer waiting for me somewhere. I just know it.

On the third day of their trip, John Henry and Polly Ann heard something. *Clang-clang. Clang-clang.* It was the sound of hammers against steel.

When they went around the next bend, they saw gangs of men. The men were driving steel spikes into the wooden ties that held the train tracks. One man in each gang knelt by the track, holding a great spike steady. Three others stood by him with hammers in their hands. *ONE-TWO-THREE*—each took a great swing. And *ONE-TWO-THREE*—their mighty blows drove the spike into the track. Then the gang moved on to another spot.

John Henry felt his heart beat in time with the blows of the hammers. This was what he was born to do. This was what he *would* do.

He went to find the foreman. "I'm a steel-driving man," John Henry said. "And I need a job."

The foreman frowned. "A steel-driving man, you say? How long have you been at it?" he asked.

"No time at all," said John Henry. "But I was born knowing how."

The foreman shook his head. "That's not good enough," he said. "Steel driving is hard and dangerous work. I need men who know what they're doing. Not beginners who might hit someone."

John Henry wasn't about to give up. Not when his dream was right before him. "Let me show you," he said. "I won't hit anyone. Why, I can drive one of those spikes all by myself."

That made the foreman laugh. "Now I'm *sure* you don't know what you're doing," he said. "No one can drive a railroad spike by himself."

"I can," said John Henry softly. "Just let me use one of your hammers."

Well, by now some of the other men had heard John Henry. They stopped working and poked one another. One of them said, "Go ahead and let him try, boss. We want to see how one man can drive a spike."

"Yes," said another. "Let's see this for ourselves."

"Fine," said the foreman. "If one of you is crazy enough to hold it for him."

Now that was a different matter. No one wanted to hold a spike for someone who didn't know what he was doing. So there was some shifting of feet. And a lot of whispering.

"I'm no fool," said one man.

"Nor am I," said another.

"I'm no fool either," said a third. "But I'll hold it for him."

The speaker stepped toward the tracks. He was a little man with a head of black, curly hair. He gave John Henry a big grin. Then he picked up a spike, bent down, and held it in place.

"It's your life, Willie," said the foreman. "But I think you're a fool."

John Henry picked up a hammer. He swung it back and forth a few times, just testing it. Then he nodded and stepped over to the spike.

Everyone was quiet, even the baby in Polly Ann's arms. Every eye was on John Henry.

John Henry started his swing. The huge hammer flashed through the air. It moved so fast that it was a blur. It moved so fast that Willie felt its wind against his cheek.

CLANG! The hammer hit the spike in the dead center. Sparks shot out as iron met steel.

"Sit back now, Willie!" shouted John Henry. Then—*CLANG!* John Henry swung again.

There was a gasp from the crowd. The spike had been driven all the way into the wood!

"Tell me your name, son," said the foreman.

"I'm John Henry," he said. "And this is my wife Polly Ann and our baby."

"Well, you've got yourself a job, John Henry," said the foreman. "And a cabin for you and your family."

At last John Henry was a steel-driving man. And the world had never seen anyone work like he did. No one was faster or more powerful. John Henry could work for ten hours without stopping. Why, before long, he started using a hammer in each hand. Then he could work twice as fast! People would come from all over just to watch.

Now the railroad tracks were heading west— right through the mountains. Those mountains were made up of hard rock. And a lot of that rock had to be moved to make way for the tracks.

So one of John Henry's jobs was driving steel drills into the rock. The drills would make a hole. Then workers could put black powder into the hole. They'd light the powder and blow the rock to pieces.

It took a lot of workers to keep up with John Henry. Why, five men were needed just to carry the steel drills he used up in one day. But only one man ever held the drills in place. That was Willie. He and John Henry were a team.

Then one day, a stranger showed up at the railroad camp. He asked for the foreman. He said, "Today is your lucky day, sir. I've got a machine that can help you. My steam drill can do the work of five men. It can make holes in solid rock so fast that your men can't keep up."

The foreman looked the salesman up and down. "Don't need it," he said at last.

"Of course you need it," said the salesman. "Why, this steam drill is the best machine ever built!"

"Don't need it," said the foreman again. "I've got John Henry. The best steel driver ever born. He can outdrill any machine."

"You think so?" said the salesman. "Well, I tell you what. We'll have a contest. A race between my machine and your man."

"What's the prize?" asked the foreman.

"If your man wins, you get my steam drill for free. If my machine wins, you buy it from me."

"Sounds fair to me," said the foreman. "But I have to check with John Henry first."

So the foreman sent someone to get John Henry. When the big man arrived, the foreman asked, "How do you feel about racing a steam drill, John Henry?"

John Henry looked at the steam drill. Then he looked at the heavy hammer in his hand. He lifted it, feeling the way the muscles bunched in his arms.

"Race a machine?" he said. "Why, a machine has no heart. It's nothing but a machine. I'll race it. And I'll beat it. Or I'll die trying."

The contest was set for the very next day. Polly Ann and Willie both tried to change John Henry's mind. But nothing they said helped. John Henry was going to race that machine.

The next morning a great crowd gathered where a tunnel was to be drilled. The steam drill was at one side. The machine gleamed in the bright sunshine. The men who ran it were busy. One was adding oil. Another was adding grease. A third was feeding the fire that made the steam and powered the drill.

John Henry and Willie stood at the other side. John Henry's bare shoulders gleamed like black coal. His hammer was in his hand.

"Are you ready?" shouted the foreman.

The steam drill salesman nodded. So did John Henry. Then the starting gun went off. The race began.

John Henry raised his hammer high into the air. *CLANG!* It hit the head of the steel drill.

At the same time, the steam drill began to roar and hiss. The drill bit into the hard rock, sending small stones flying.

John Henry didn't pay any attention to the

machine. He just kept swinging. Over and over, he lifted the hammer high. Over and over, he brought it smashing down on the head of the steel drills.

On one side, men rushed to tend to the machine. On the other side, they rushed to bring new steel drills for Willie to hold. And to pour cold water on John Henry's hammer. He was working so hard that the great hammer was smoking.

The steam drill hissed and roared. John Henry's hammer clanged and banged. Clouds of steam rose into the air. Rivers of sweat poured down John Henry's back and arms.

At the end of an hour the machine was ahead. "Bring me another hammer, Willie!" shouted John Henry. "I'm just getting started! I'm not even tired yet!"

A hammer in each hand, John Henry went back to work. He swung those hammers so fast that no one could see them. All they could see were the sparks made when a hammer hit a spike.

Inch by inch, the steam drill made one hole in the mountainside.

Inch by inch, John Henry made another.

For a time the machine stayed ahead. Then the drill broke and had to be replaced. So John Henry was ahead.

It went on like that all morning and all

afternoon. First the drill would be ahead. Then John Henry. Then the drill.

"The machine's going to win!" some shouted.

"John Henry's going to win!" shouted others.

John Henry didn't stop to rest. He just kept swinging. His heart thundered in his chest. A roar filled his ears. The noise of the steam drill, he thought.

The sun began to sink in the sky. As the last rays slid behind the mountain, there was the sound of a shot. The race was over!

"You won, John Henry!" shouted the railroad foreman. "You beat the machine!"

John Henry stood there, leaning on a hammer. He nodded once, then fell to the ground.

Willie and Polly Ann both rushed to his side. John Henry opened his eyes and smiled at them. "I was a real steel-driving man, wasn't I?" he said. Then he closed his eyes forever.

John Henry's story was told many times after that. The story of how a man with a big heart beat a machine with a big engine.

And even today, if you listen closely, you can hear the sound of John Henry's hammer. You can hear it in the *click-clack* of the trains as they head down the tracks.

JOHN HENRY

The Play

Cast of Characters

Narrator

Mama Henry

Polly Ann

Worker 1

Willie

John Henry

Papa Henry

Foreman

Worker 2

Salesman

Setting: America during and after the Civil War

Act One

Narrator: John Henry was born to be a steel-driving man. Everyone could see it.

Mama Henry: Papa! Look at what little John is doing!

Papa Henry: Why, he's swinging that hammer! He's swinging it higher and faster than I can. And I'm a grown man.

Mama Henry: I think our boy is going to be a steel-driving man. He's going to work on the railroads.

Papa Henry: Don't be silly, Mama. John Henry is going to pick cotton on the plantation. Just like you do. Just like I do. He can't choose what he wants to do. He's a slave.

Narrator: John Henry's papa was right. But that didn't stop John Henry from dreaming. And the older he got, the stronger the dreams were. One day John Henry went to his parents.

John Henry: Papa, Mama, I had a dream.

Mama Henry: What did you dream about, John Henry?

John Henry: I was listening to the trains, Mama. And I was dreaming about driving steel for the railroads.

Papa Henry: It's plain to see that you were born to be a steel-driving man, son. But you're a slave. You can't leave the plantation.

John Henry: I know that, Papa. But it's a powerful dream I had. And there's more to it.

Mama Henry: More?

John Henry: Yes. I dreamed that I'd die with a hammer in my hand.

Papa Henry: Enough of that talk, son.

Narrator: So John Henry didn't say any more about his dream. But his mama and papa didn't forget about it. And neither did John Henry. Not even when he met Polly Ann. Not even when he fell in love with her.

John Henry: I have strong feelings for you, Polly Ann.

Polly Ann: I care for you too, John Henry.

John Henry:	But I have to tell you something. I aim to be a steel-driving man someday. That's my dream.
Polly Ann:	Then it's my dream too.
Narrator:	So John Henry and Polly Ann were married. And soon they had a fine, strapping son of their own.
	Not long after that the war ended. Things were changing in the South.
John Henry:	The war is over! We're free, Polly Ann! Free!
Polly Ann:	Our son won't grow up to be a slave!
John Henry:	This means I can do what I've always dreamed about, Polly Ann. I can be a steel-driving man.
Polly Ann:	Where will you go?
John Henry:	West, that's where. They're building a great railroad out there, Polly Ann. And that's where I'm going. For I was born to be a steel-driving man.
Polly Ann:	I'm coming with you. And so is our baby.
John Henry:	Then we'll leave tomorrow.

Act Two

Narrator: So John Henry, Polly Ann, and their baby set out the very next day.

John Henry: There's a hammer waiting for me somewhere. I just know it.

Polly Ann: You'll find it, John Henry. You were born to be a steel-driving man.

Narrator: They walked for three days, always heading west.

Polly Ann: I hear something! A clanging sound!

John Henry: So do I! It sounds like hammers hitting steel. And I think it's coming from just around the bend.

Narrator: John Henry was right. When they rounded the bend, they could see gangs of men at work. The men were driving steel spikes into the wooden ties that held the train tracks. One man in each gang knelt by the track, holding a great spike steady. Three others stood by him with hammers in their hands. *ONE-TWO-THREE*—each took a great swing. And *ONE-TWO-THREE*—their mighty blows drove the spike into the track. Then the gang moved on to another spot.

John Henry: Look at that, Polly Ann! And listen! My heart is beating in time with the hammers. This is what I was born to do.

Polly Ann: I think that man over there is the foreman. You can ask him for work.

John Henry: Mr. Foreman? Mr. Foreman?

Foreman: Yes? What can I do for you, young man?

John Henry: I'm a steel-driving man, sir. And I need a job.

Foreman: A steel-driving man, you say? How long have you been at it?

John Henry: No time at all. But I was born knowing how.

Foreman: That's not good enough. Steel driving is hard work. And dangerous work. I need men who know what they're doing.

Worker 1: He's right. We don't need any beginners. You'll hit someone.

John Henry: Mr. Foreman, just let me show you. I won't hit anyone. Why, I can drive one of those spikes all by myself.

Foreman: Now I'm *sure* you don't know what you're doing. No one can drive a railroad spike by himself.

John Henry: I can. If you'll let me use one of your hammers.

Worker 2: Go ahead and let him try, boss. I want to see how one man can drive a spike all by himself.

Worker 1: Yes. Let's see this for ourselves.

Foreman: Fine. If one of you is crazy enough to hold it for him.

Worker 2: Not me!

Worker 1: Nor me. I'm no fool.

Willie: I'm no fool either. But I'll hold it for him.

Worker 2: You *are* a fool, Willie.

Foreman: It's your life. Go ahead and hold it.

Narrator: So Willie stepped up and gave John Henry a big grin. Then he picked up a spike, bent down, and held it in place.

John Henry: Thank you kindly.

Willie: Just hit the spike. That'll be thanks enough for me.

Polly Ann: You can do it. I know you can.

Narrator: John Henry picked up a hammer. He swung it back and forth a few times, just testing it. Then he nodded and stepped over to the spike.

Everyone was quiet, even the baby in Polly Ann's arms. Every eye was on John Henry.

John Henry: Sit back, Willie!

Worker 1: He's starting to swing!

Worker 2: Look at that hammer go! I can hardly see it!

Worker 1: I can feel the wind from it though!

Narrator: The hammer hit the spike in the dead center! Then John Henry swung again.

Polly Ann: You did it!

Willie: He did it! He drove the spike in with only two blows!

Foreman: Amazing! What's your name, son?

John Henry: I'm John Henry. This is my wife Polly Ann and our baby boy.

Foreman: Well, you've got yourself a job, John Henry. And a cabin for you and your family.

John Henry: I'm a steel-driving man at last!

<u>Act Three</u>

Narrator: John Henry was truly a steel-driving man. And the world had never seen anyone work like he did. No one was faster or more powerful.

Worker 1: That John Henry can work for ten hours without stopping.

Worker 2: And he uses a hammer in each hand!

Narrator: Now the railroad tracks were heading west—right through the mountains. Those mountains were made up of hard rock. And a lot of that rock had to be moved to make way for the tracks. So one of John Henry's jobs was driving steel drills into the rock.

Worker 1: We can hardly keep up with him. It takes five men just to carry the steel drills he uses up in a day.

Willie: And I'm the only one who holds them in place for him. John Henry and I are a team.

Narrator: The whole railroad camp was a team. But John Henry was their leader. As fast as the wooden ties were put down, he pounded in spikes. Every day the tracks headed farther and farther west.

Willie: Now we've got to go through the mountains.

John Henry: We can do it, Willie. You hold the steel drills, and I'll hammer them in.

Worker 1: Then I'll stuff black powder in the hole.

Worker 2: And I'll light it. We'll blow the rock to pieces!

Willie: Before you know it, we'll be on the other side of the mountain.

Narrator: And that's what they did. Day after day. Week after week. A lot of rock had to be moved to make way for the tracks.

Then one day a stranger showed up at the railroad camp.

Salesman: Say, where's the foreman of this camp? I need to talk to him.

Foreman: I'm the foreman. What can I do for you?

Salesman: No, the question is, what can *I* do for you? Today is your lucky day!

Foreman: Why's that?

Salesman: I've got a machine that can help you. My steam drill can do the work of five men. It can make holes in solid rock so fast that your men can't keep up.

Foreman: Don't need it.

Salesman: Of course you need it. Why this steam drill is the best machine ever built!

Foreman: Don't need it, I said. I've got John Henry. The best steel driver ever born. He can outdrill any machine.

Salesman: You think so? Well, I tell you what. We'll have a contest. A race between my machine and your man.

Foreman: What's the prize?

Salesman: If your man wins, you get my steam drill for free. If my machine wins, you buy it from me.

Foreman: Sounds fair. But I'll have to check with John Henry first. Willie, run and get him.

John Henry: You wanted to see me, boss?

Foreman: How do you feel about racing a steam drill, John Henry?

John Henry: Race a machine? Why, a machine has no heart. It's nothing but a machine. I'll race it. And I'll beat it. Or I'll die trying.

Polly Ann: No, John Henry. Don't do it.

Willie: She's right, John Henry.

John Henry: I'm going to do it. And I'm going to win.

Salesman: We'll have the race tomorrow.

Narrator: The next morning a great crowd gathered where a tunnel was to be drilled. The steam drill was at one side, gleaming in the bright sunshine. The men who ran it were busy. One was adding oil. Another was adding grease. A third was feeding the fire that made the steam and powered the drill.

Willie: It's not too late to change your mind, John Henry.

John Henry: I'm not changing my mind, Willie.

Foreman: Are you ready?

Salesman: We're ready.

John Henry: So are we.

Foreman: Go!

Narrator: John Henry raised his hammer high into the air. *CLANG!* It hit the head of the steel drill. At the same time, the steam drill began to roar and hiss. The drill bit into the hard rock, sending small stones flying.

Salesman: Water! Bring some more water for the steam drill!

Worker 1: Bring some new drills for Willie to hold!

Worker 2: And pour some water on John Henry's hammer! It's smoking!

Narrator: The steam drill hissed and roared. John Henry's hammer clanged and banged. Clouds of steam rose into the air. Rivers of sweat poured down John Henry's back and arms.

John Henry: It's been an hour, Willie. How are we doing?

Willie: The steam drill is ahead.

John Henry: Bring me another hammer! I'm just getting started!

Polly Ann: No, John Henry!

John Henry: I'm not even tired yet!

Worker 1: Here's another hammer, John Henry.

Narrator:	John Henry went back to work. He swung those hammers so fast that no one could see them. All they could see were the sparks made when a hammer hit a spike.
Salesman:	The drill broke! Quick! Replace it!
Worker 2:	You're ahead now, John Henry! Keep it up!
Salesman:	Now we're ahead! We're going to win!
Worker 1:	John Henry's going to win!
Willie:	How are you doing, John Henry?
John Henry:	My heart is thundering, Willie. And I hear a roar. It must be the steam drill.
Narrator:	The sun began to sink in the sky. As the last rays slid behind the mountain, there was the sound of a shot.
Polly Ann:	It's over! The race is over!
Foreman:	You won, John Henry! You beat the machine.
Willie:	John Henry! What's the matter?
Foreman:	He's falling!

Polly Ann: Let me get to him. Oh, John Henry!

John Henry: I was a real steel-driving man, wasn't I, Polly Ann? But now I have to say good-bye.

Willie: Hold on, John Henry!

Foreman: It's too late, Willie. He's dead.

Polly Ann: He died with a hammer in his hand. Just like he said he would.

Narrator: John Henry's story was told many times after that. It was the story of how a man with a big heart beat a machine with a big engine. And even today if you listen closely, you can hear the sound of John Henry's hammer. You can hear it in the *click-clack* of the trains as they head down the tracks.